How Mrs. Santa Claus
Saved Christmas

How Mrs. Santa Claus
Saved Christmas

By PHYLLIS McGINLEY

Drawings by KURT WERTH

J. B. LIPPINCOTT COMPANY

Philadelphia • New York

Everybody knows how Santa Claus looks.

You've seen his picture in your picture books.
You've heard about his house
(With the North Pole near)
And his sack
And his sleigh
And his eight reindeer.
But did you ever before in your life
Know Santa Claus had a wife?

Well, he has.
She's the reason he doesn't get thinner,
For she serves his breakfast,
She cooks his dinner,
She warms his slippers and dries his boots
And mends the fur
On his Santa Claus suits.

And what is she like?
By best report
She's a cozy,
Rosy
Grandmotherly sort
With a dimple in her cheek,
A twinkle in her eye,
And a smell of vanilla
And hot mince pie.
But the nicest thing that I've heard about her
Is:
Santa couldn't get on without her.

For it may be Santa Claus who makes toys for all the children in the world. It may be Santa Claus who drives his sleigh through the winter sky and climbs down waiting chimneys. But it's Mrs. Claus who gives him his Good Ideas.

"Santa," she'll tell him in mid-November,
"There's a brand-new boy at the Smiths,
        remember.
He ought to have something that's just his size,
Say, a nice blue rattle the color of his eyes.
And Haverford Jones, now—
Don't forget
He's pining for a grown-up
Chemistry set.
His parents pretend that it can't be done.
But I *like* Haverford.
Bring him one."

She knows when children in the State of Maine
Are ready for their first electric train;
Or she'll say briskly,
"On Earth, I hear,
Dresses for ladies
Are short this year.
So don't you think that the fashion calls
For shorter dresses on little girls' dolls?"

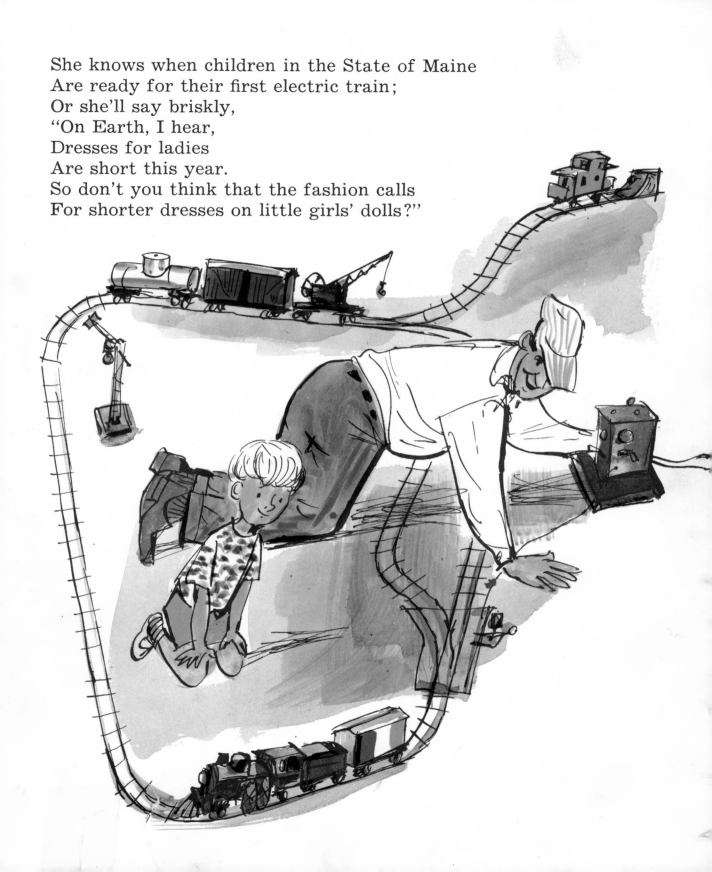

And Santa hems
And Santa haws
But he usually listens
To Mrs. Claus . . .
Except just once
When they couldn't agree
And this is the story as it came to me:

It was Christmas Eve at the end of day.
The reindeer nickered as they champed their hay.
Elbows flying, the reindeer Groom
Polished up the harness
In the big store room
While Santa, weary from the wear and tear
Lounged by the fire in his easy chair.

"I think," he murmured
With pardonable pride,
"Everything is ready for my Midnight Ride.

"Everything's jolly as it's always been.
The sleigh stands waiting,
With gifts crammed in—
Tricycles,
Bicycles,
Dump-truck toys
And cowboy outfits for a million boys;
Jump ropes,
Jackstones,
Dolls with curls
And sets of dishes for a million girls;
Books for the bookish
Who sit and read,
Baseball mitts for the baseball breed,
Kites for the tomboy, or balls to pitch,
Practical presents
For the not-so-rich,
Candy for the sweet tooth,
Chess for the clever.

It's just as it's been forever and ever.
I do think Christmas will be fine this year.
Don't you agree with that,
My dear?"

Mrs. Claus was washing up the dinner dishes and stacking them in the china closet. She wiped her hands on her apron, turned around to Santa and looked at him over her spectacles. And then she said firmly, "No." Santa was so surprised, he nearly fell off his chair into the fire.

"No," she said in the clearest of voices,
"I'm tired of our
Same old,
Tame old
Choices.
Maybe you'll consider
That my plans are strange,
But just one Christmas, let's have
A change."

"Change?" asked Santa
In a startled way.

Said she,
"I thought of it just today.
We don't want the Helpers to overhear
So come a little closer.
I'll whisper in your ear."

Up on her toes stood Mrs. C.
And "Buzz . . . buzz . . . buzz . . ."
Like a honey bee,
"Buzz, buzz, buzz"
Like a bee in clover
She whispered her secret over and over.

But Santa Claus's look got blacker and blacker.
His breath came "pop"
Like a red fire-cracker.
His whiskers wiggled,
His lip drew down,
He put on his terrible Santa Claus frown,
Then,
"Stop," he thundered,
"Not one word more!"
And he stamped from his chair to the bedroom
      door.
"Me, change Christmas?
Why, what a question!
It's given me sneezes and indigestion,
A pain in my shoulder,
A rash, a cough.
I *must* have a nap to sleep it off.
It's hours till midnight
By the clock on the shelf.
Let nobody wake me.
I'll wake myself."

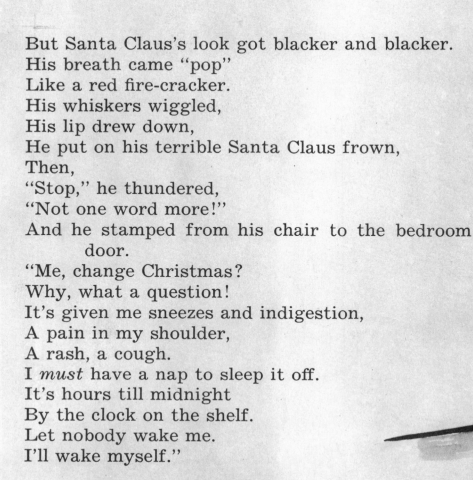

    And he went indignantly into his room, muttering, "I never heard of such nonsense!" The door shut behind him and Mrs. Claus heard the bed creak as he threw himself down upon it. She finished sweeping up the kitchen and then sat calmly down with her crocheting. The clock ticked on and on and on. Soon it was twelve o'clock and Santa hadn't stirred.

At ten past twelve the reindeer Groom
Phoned Mrs. Claus from the big storeroom:
"Please tell Santa the reindeer wait
While children dream in their beds.
He's late!
Already the stars are a silver warning.
Doesn't he know it's Christmas morning?"

"Tap," she tapped at the bedroom door,
"Tap, tap, tap" and one "tap" more.
But poor tired Santa, worn to a splinter,
Slept like a bear holed up for winter,
Slept like a porcupine
Curled in a Q.
What was a wife to do?

Do not disturb

She put down her needle, she wound her thread.
She gave one toss of her merry head,
Then half to herself said,
"This may shake him,
But didn't he tell me I shouldn't wake him?
I have the addresses,
I know the way,
And *somebody* has to drive that
Sleigh!"

On went a muffler about her throat.
On went the big red fur-trimmed coat.
(Though it seemed like a giant's size too wide,
She belted it round her,
A pillow inside.)
On went the big boots,
On went the cap.
She picked up gloves and the Christmas map,
And rummaged in a cupboard
Till she found therein
A false set of whiskers
To fasten on her chin,
Till you couldn't have told
With a casual stare
That it wasn't Santa Claus standing there.

And maybe the reindeer sensed the change,
And maybe the Groom may have thought it strange
That never a word passed Santa's lip
As he climbed in the sleigh and cracked the whip,
But long before they could ask or pause,
Into the air
Flew Mrs. Claus.

Dawn was coloring the sky when Santa woke. He rubbed his eyes, looked at his watch and leaped from bed as if he had been stung by a hive of hornets. "I've missed the Ride," he shouted. And he began to ring every bell in the place. Elves and Gnomes came running from all parts of the house, half dressed, half asleep, and very frightened indeed. They could *not* understand what he was storming about.

"By the Stars in the Dipper!
By the Milky Way!
Who let me sleep till Christmas Day?
A thousand years and never a miss,
But how can children
Forgive me this?
I'm ruined!
I'm finished!
And all because
They'll give up depending
On Santa Claus!"

"But, Sir," cried the Groom,
"It can't be so!
I waved goodbye to you hours ago
With the deer and the sleigh and the gift-crammed
            pack
And . . .
There you are now, Sir . . .
Coming back!"

His mouth fell open with a foolish grin
As the reindeer team came jingling in
And gay as a sparrow (though twice as stout)
A little red figure climbed stiffly out.

"I must admit
They were hard on me—
All those chimneys,"
Said Mrs. C.

The Saint was taken by such surprise
He could merely mumble
And blink his eyes.
Then he roared so loud that the roof got quivery,
"You mean to say
That *you*
Made delivery?
You drove my reindeer?
You steered the sleigh?
Then heaven help children
On Earth today!"

"Now, Santa," Mrs. Claus said quietly, "wait till I get this big old coat off and I'll explain." And she pulled him down into his chair. "After all, you told me most particularly that I wasn't to wake you up."

"Though now that you've asked me,
I must confess
It's an odd sort of Christmas,
More or less.
I wasn't quite sure how you had things fixed up.
Maybe I got the addresses mixed up,
Yet anyhow, Santa,"
She said, and smiled,
"I did leave a present for every child:
Skis for the bookworms,
Books to read
On rainy Sundays
For the Baseball Breed;
For girls who had nothing but dolls on hand,
Nice red dump-trucks for dumping sand;
Nice soft Pandas, huggable and fat
For little boys waiting
For a cowboy hat;

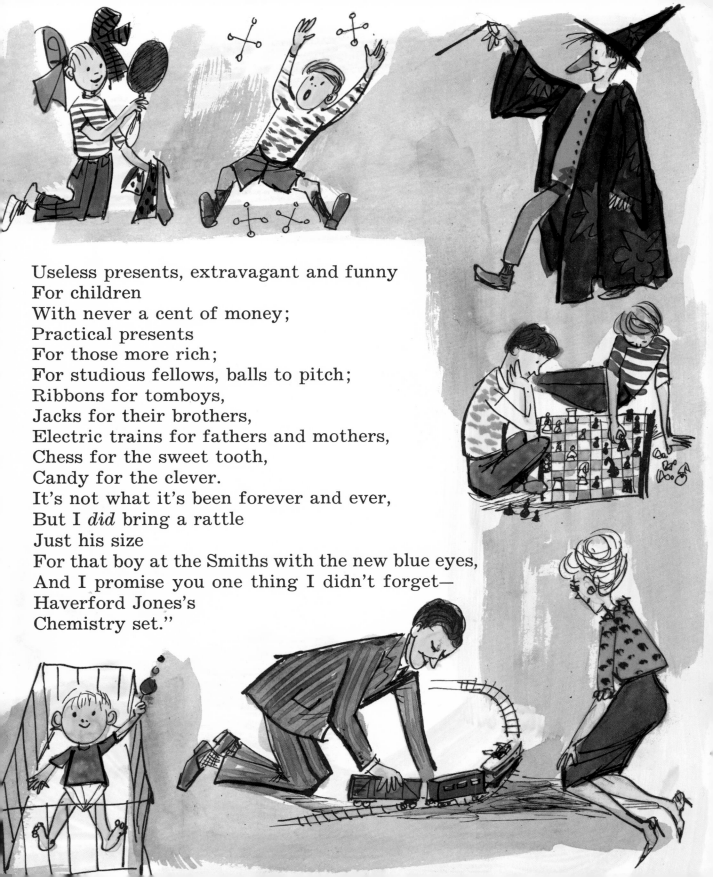

Useless presents, extravagant and funny
For children
With never a cent of money;
Practical presents
For those more rich;
For studious fellows, balls to pitch;
Ribbons for tomboys,
Jacks for their brothers,
Electric trains for fathers and mothers,
Chess for the sweet tooth,
Candy for the clever.
It's not what it's been forever and ever,
But I *did* bring a rattle
Just his size
For that boy at the Smiths with the new blue eyes,
And I promise you one thing I didn't forget—
Haverford Jones's
Chemistry set."

"Alas," moaned Santa,
Hands to his face.
"I'll never recover from this disgrace.
Glance at the earth,
You're sure to see
Children crying by the Christmas tree,
Children sobbing till they wet their sleeve,
For gifts expected
They didn't receive.
Listen. You hear them?"

And leagues around,
Up from the world
Came a curious sound,
A sound like the surge of waves on a shore,
First a ripple and then a roar
Till the North Pole trembled both fore and after.
But it wasn't weeping.
It was children's laughter—
Giggles and gales and peals of mirth
From startled children around the earth,
Gusts of merriment,
Cheers,
Applause,
And a chorus of
"Thank you, Santa Claus,
For bringing last night through the dark and cold,
The wish of our hearts
We had never told."

Santa stared at Mrs. Claus for a long, long time without a word. Suddenly he began to laugh, too. He laughed so hard that she had to tap him on the back for fear he would choke. He laughed so loud that he sent snow sliding down the window panes. When he could speak once more he said stoutly, "Merry Christmas!" And Mrs. Claus said, "Merry Christmas," back.

"By the Wild North Wind!"
He chuckled then,
"I can take a joke with the best of men.
We needed a change, or I'm a dunce.
All right, my dear, we have had it.
Once.
But after this leave the Ride to me."

"I'll be delighted,"
Said Mrs. C.

And they and the Helpers sat down to a breakfast of bacon and eggs and sausages and fried chicken and hot cakes with maple syrup and two kinds of rolls and marmalade and currant jelly and plum pudding. But Mrs. Claus was so tired out from chimney-climbing that Santa had to get supper that night for himself.

JP   SOUTH AMHERST   copy 3
     McGinley, Phyllis
          How Mrs. Santa Claus
saved Christmas   DEC 26 1986

MAY - 7 1974   DEC 13 1978

NOV 5 - 1974   JAN 22 1997

DEC 16 1974   DEC 14 1979

JAN 3   1975   JAN 18 1980

JAN - 6 1976   DEC 22 1980

DEC 21 1976

JAN - 4 1977   JAN 18 1984
DEC 14 1977   DEC 26 1984
12/29/77

DEC 16 1987   JAN 5 1988
DEC 19 1982
NOV 23 1984   DEC 28 1989
                     DEC 29 1988
DEC 12 1994   DEC 27 1994
                     DEC 26 1995